Gedalia The Goldfish

Who Wanted To Be Just Like The King

by **Miriam Yerushalmi**
illustrated by
Devorah Weinberg

First Edition - Adar 5767 / March 2007

ISBN: 0-911643-36-2

Writer's Press Brooklyn, New York
A division of **Aura Printing** 88 Parkville Ave., Brooklyn, NY 11230 718-435-9103

Printed in China

Once upon a time, there was a beautiful goldfish, named Gedalia. He lived near the palace of a very righteous king. Everyday, Gedalia would watch the king whom he admired for all his acts of kindness and wisdom. He wanted to be just like the king and decided to imitate his good deeds.

One morning, he watched the king pray to Hashem. "The king is
so humble and grateful," Gedalia thought to himself. "I also want to
pray to Hashem, but I do not have hands to cover my eyes for
Shema, nor do I have knees to bend and bow to Hashem for the
Shemone Esray prayer."
He started to feel a bit frustrated, but then he had a wonderful idea.

"I know, I can use my fins to cover my eyes, and I'll do a flip for my bow," he said to himself. He was so excited he couldn't wait to begin.

And so Gedalia began praying to Hashem. He looked so cute bowing in the water. But, most importantly, Gedalia meant every word he said. When Gedalia finished praying, he said, "That felt so good. Now I feel just like the king."

After praying, the king was already busy with another Mitzvah. The king stepped out into the fields to give Tzedaka to the poor people.

"I want to be kind and compassionate just like the king," Gedalia thought. "How can I give Tzedaka? I have no gold coins to give charity with."

He pondered and then came up with a brilliant idea. He jumped quickly into the water and began searching for pearls. Soon after, he found the most gorgeous pearls.

"I can exchange these pearls with my friend the fisherman for money and give it to a poor family," he said to himself.

After he had collected a sack full of pearls, he went to the fisherman who sat in his little boat every morning.

"Would you be interested in exchanging this sack of pearls for some gold coins?" Gedalia asked him.

"Let me see what you've got there," the Fisherman said to Gedalia, as he took the sack of pearls and examined them. "These are very fine pearls," he told Gedalia. "I can offer you 100 gold coins for the whole sack if you are interested."

"I am very interested," replied Gedalia, "but I have one special request. Would you be able to make a small necklace that could fit a fish? I know a special fish that would be so happy to receive a pearl necklace."

"I think I could do that for you," the fisherman replied. He selected twelve small pearls from the sack and strung them with his fishing wire. "Here you are," he told Gedalia as he handed him the gold coins and pearl necklace. "It was nice to see you again. Please come and visit me any time," the fisherman told Gedalia.

"I would love to," Gedalia told him excitedly. "Thank you for helping me do an important Mitzvah." Gedalia was overjoyed!

As he swam back into the water he noticed a shipwreck. Gedalia saw that a poor widow with her nine baby guppies lived inside. He knocked on the door and the widow welcomed him in. As soon as he entered, Gedalia realized that he had come to the right place. He had never been in a shipwreck before. He immediately gave the widow the coins and she was very grateful.

Seeing the bag of gold coins made her feel blessed again. Suddenly, she did not feel so alone. She then said, "I don't know how I can ever thank you,"

"Please don't thank me. Give thanks to Hashem. He is the source of all that is good. And besides, I need to thank you for letting me have the opportunity to do the Mitzvah of Tzedaka," replied Gedalia.

Gedalia blew kisses to the guppy children and swam on his way. "I feel so happy," he thought to himself. "I feel just like the king."

Gedalia swam as fast as he could and as soon as he arrived near the palace, he jumped out of the water to see what the king was doing next. Now the king was doing the Mitzvah of Bikur Cholim. He was visiting an old sickly man and feeding him a bowl of soup.

"It is so nice to see a great king interrupting his busy schedule to feed an old man. I also want to do the Mitzvah of Bikur Cholim," Gedalia thought. "I don't know of any sick fish in the water, but maybe I should look around. You never know," he added.

As he dived back into the water, he saw a little fish whose fin was caught under a rock. The little fish cried out,

"Will somebody please help me? I'm stuck! I'm hungry! I haven't eaten all day!"

Gedalia swam towards the little fish to free his fin from under the rock. As Gedalia moved the heavy rock, he said encouragingly,

"Never lose hope my little friend, I am here to help you."

As Gedalia helped free the little fish, he noticed a little wound. Gedalia then wrapped the wound with a waterproof bandage.

"Don't worry; I'll take good care of you. Rest here while I fix you something to eat." Gedalia then asked, "Do you like seaweed soup?"

"That is my favorite soup! How did you know?" asked the little fish.

"Just a lucky guess," answered Gedalia, as he began to prepare the soup. When the soup was ready, he fed the little fish.

"That was delicious! I don't know how to thank you," the little fish told him as he sipped the last drops.

"It is I who have to thank you for letting me have the opportunity to do the Mitzvah of Bikur Cholim," Gedalia responded. "Rest now and later I'll come again and check up on you," Gedalia added. As soon as the little fish fell asleep, Gedalia said, "I feel so good. I feel just like the king."

Gedalia swam to the palace to see what the king was doing next. He saw two people arguing with each other in front of the king. The king then settled their case and made peace between them. Gedalia was very impressed.

"The way the king settled that dispute was ingenious," he thought. "From now on, I am going to try to be a peacemaker."

As he was swimming with this thought in mind, he noticed his two friends Shmuel the Salmon and Tuvia the Trout arguing over a shell. Shmuel the Salmon was yelling,

"I found this shell first. It's mine!"

Tuvia the Trout yelled back, "No, you are wrong, I found this shell first. I left it here earlier! It's mine, give it back to me!"

Gedalia the Goldfish spoke up and said to them, "My, my, both of you seem really upset over this shell. You know what is more important than that shell? Your friendship. Don't you two remember the Mitzvah of VeAhavta Le'Rei'acha Kamocha, of loving your friend like yourself? Besides, look around you, there are plenty of shells around here. Now, I want you to remember all the good times the two of you have shared together."

"You are absolutely right! How could we have been so foolish!" said Shmuel.

"Yeah! What's a shell compared to our friendship!" said Tuvia.

They hugged each other right away and said together, "Thank you so much, Gedalia!"

Gedalia hugged them both and responded kindly, "Really I must thank you for giving me the opportunity to do the Mitzvah of Hava'as Shalom Ben Adam LeChavero, bringing peace between friends."

Gedalia the Goldfish left feeling very happy. "Now I feel more like the king," he told himself.

When he arrived at the water's edge to see what the king was doing next, he couldn't believe his eyes. It was a most beautiful sight! The king was building a beautiful shul.

Gedalia thought to himself, "How spectacular! If only I could help! But how? I know! I'll gather precious stones to help build the Shul."

He started collecting the most beautiful stones he could find. After he had gathered a large collection, he left them at the water's edge with a note on them saying, "Precious stones for the Shul."

Gedalia had no doubt that the king would find them, because every evening he would pass that same spot on his way home to the palace. Gedalia quickly jumped back into the water and waited.

The king did pass the water's edge and noticed the beautiful stones. As he read the note, he wondered to himself, "Who donated these precious stones for the Shul? I really would like to thank him personally."

He saw a fisherman nearby and asked, "Do you know who collected these precious stones?"

"Your Majesty, I am sorry but I don't," the fisherman's replied.

Gedalia was so excited to hear the king's voice. He jumped out of the water and, to the king's amazement, he exclaimed, "It was I!"

The king was surprised to find out that it was a fish who donated the precious stones for the Shul. Gedalia then began relating,

"I always watch you from a distance and admire the Mitzvahs you do. I want to be just like you. When I saw you building the Shul, I wanted to join you in making a house for Hashem."

"What a special little goldfish you are. Thank you for your kind words." Gedalia then blushed. The king then asked "May I have the honor of taking you to my own pond back at the Palace, so you can become the royal goldfish?"

"It would be my honor," Gedalia exclaimed with a big smile."

The king scooped Gedalia the Goldfish into a golden goblet and said,

"Before I bring you to my private pond, I would like you to come with me and watch me put these precious stones that you collected into the Shul."

"I am so happy to accompany you, Gedalia squealed. The king carried Gedalia and the precious stones to the Shul. Gedalia watched with great joy as the king placed the stones in the Shul. They were so bright they sparkled with a G-dly light.

The king then carried Gedalia back to the palace. Gedalia loved his new home. He especially liked waking up in the morning and hearing the king pray, sing his Tehillim and learn Torah. And there were always opportunities to do many Mitzvahs together.

Gedalia was so thankful to Hashem for his new
friendship with the king. He was the happiest fish in the
whole world because now he was so close to the king.